Sweet Jasmine, Nice Jackson

by ROBIE H. HARRIS

illustrated by MICHAEL EMBERLEY

MARGARET K. McELDERRY BOOKS

NEW YORK   LONDON   TORONTO   SYDNEY

Margaret K. McElderry Books
An imprint of Simon & Schuster Children's Publishing Division
1230 Avenue of the Americas, New York, NY 10020

Text copyright © 2004 by Bee Productions, Inc.
Illustrations copyright © 2004 by Bird Productions, Inc.

Book design by Sonia Chaghatzbanian
The text of this book is set in Lucida Casual.
The illustrations are rendered in watercolor, pastel, and pen and ink.

"Happy Birthday to You," by Mildred J. Hill and Patty S. Hill, ©1935 (renewed) by Summy-Birchard
Music, a division of Summy-Birchard, Inc. All rights reserved. Used by permission.
Warner Bros. Publications U.S. Inc. Miami, FL 33014

Manufactured in China
2 4 6 8 10 9 7 5 3 1
LIBRARY OF CONGRESS CATALOGING-IN-PUBLICATION DATA
Harris, Robie H.
Sweet Jasmine, Nice Jackson : what it's like to be 2—and to be twins! / by Robie H. Harris ;
illustrated by Michael Emberley.—1st ed.
p. cm. — (Growing up stories ; 3)
Summary: Jasmine and Jackson celebrate the year they are two by learning to do new things and
showing their independence. Includes nonfiction information about two-year-olds and twins.
ISBN 0-689-83259-1 (hardcover)
[1. Twins—Fiction. 2. Toddlers—Fiction.] I. Emberley, Michael, ill.
II. Title.
PZ7.H2436 Sw 2004
[E]—dc21
2002152902

FIRST
EDITION

For ELLA! For SAM! For the 2 of YOU!—Love you both!
—R. H. H.

For Roberta,
my creative twin sister
—M. E.

Two-year-olds grow up in many different kinds of families—families with one child; families with two, three, four, or more children; and families with twins, or triplets, or sometimes quadruplets, quintuplets, sextuplets, or septuplets.

Jasmine and Jackson were **2**. They were 2 years old. There were 2 of them. And they were twins. The morning after their second birthday, Jackson stood up in his crib and sang, "Me here, Jassie-Jassie!"

"Me here, Jackie-Jackie!" sang Jasmine back. Soon, their daddy came and lifted them out of their cribs. And as their feet touched the floor they hugged each other, fell in a heap—and hugged again!

Later that morning, Jackson banged his drum and sang, "Me do it! Jackie do it!" Jasmine tried to bang the drum too. But when Jackson pushed her away, she cried, "Me do it! Jassie do it do it!"

"Okay, Jassie, okay!" said Jackson. "Go do it!" And he let her bang the drum.

When two babies are born from the same mommy's body at almost the same time, they are called "twins." When twins are born, first one twin is born, then the other twin is born. Twins are usually born anywhere from a few minutes apart to thirty minutes or so apart. Sometimes it can take longer.

Twins can be two girls, or two boys, or one boy and one girl. Some twins do not look like each other. Other twins look almost exactly alike. Two-year-old twins–just like other two-year-olds–haven't learned to share or take turns very well yet. But they are beginning to know that sharing a toy is a nice thing to do.

ME HERE, JACKIE-JACKIE!

The next morning when their mommy asked, "Time for a new diaper?" Jasmine shouted, "NO! NO dipe! NO-NO-NO-NOOOO!" and ran out of the room. Mommy waved a new diaper in the air—one with bunnies on it. When Jasmine saw the bunnies, she whispered, "Oh, bunny!" and let Mommy put the new diaper on her.

That night when their Daddy said, "Time to go night-night!" Jackson whispered, "NO night-night!"—and ran out of the room. After Daddy tucked him in bed, read him a story, hugged him, kissed him, and turned out the light, Jackson still whispered, "NO night-night! NO Daddy! NO-no-no-no-oooo-oooo-oooo . . . ," until he fell asleep.

I GET THE BALL!

NO! DON'T DO THAT!

Two-year-olds hear the word "NO!" a lot. And they say "NO!" a lot. They even say "NO!" to their toys and pets. Saying "NO!" is their way of telling someone, "I want to do what I want to do!" Later on, they do learn that they can't always do what they want to do—or have what they want to have.

Many people still call two-year-olds "toddlers" even though they don't "toddle"—take short, wobbly steps—anymore. Now they can walk faster, take bigger and less wobbly steps, run faster, climb higher and faster, jump and hop, kick a ball, and walk up and down stairs. Most two-year-olds still wear diapers. Some older two-year-olds may begin to wear underpants.

HOP-HOP-HOPPITY-HOP!

A few weeks later, when Daddy put shaving cream on Jackson's face, he pretended to shave—just like Daddy. Then Daddy brushed his teeth and spit in the sink. Jackson brushed his teeth and spit in the sink too—just like Daddy. After breakfast, Daddy put on his baseball cap. Jackson put on his cap and wore it backwards—just like Daddy.

Some two-year-olds try to take off their clothes—their T-shirt, shoes and socks, or hats and gloves—at home or even when they're out. Others—at home, or at a friend's house, or at the park—may even try to take off their diaper. They think dressing and undressing themselves is fun and feel so proud when they can finally do it—no matter where they are or how they look.

MOM!
HE'S DOING IT AGAIN!

I THINK THAT'S ENOUGH MILK!!!

WHY?

Two-year-olds are always trying to do things on their own—pouring milk or zipping a zipper—even when they can't do what they want to do. Doing or trying to do something on their own is one way they learn to do new things. Sometimes they get very mad or even cry when they can't do something all on their own.

Soon, when Jackson got dressed, he didn't want any help—even when he needed help. Sometimes he put both feet into the same pant leg and had to start over again. Other times, he put his rain boots on the wrong feet and wore them that way—all day long. After he dressed himself, Jackson loved to look in the mirror and shout, "Look good! Jackie look good!"

Two-year-olds love to look at, play with, hug, kiss, and talk to babies. Maybe that's because they can do so many more things than babies can and that makes them feel good—or because they were babies only a short time ago and remember how good it felt, and still feels, to be cuddled and held.

SMOOCH!

OK. OK. I FORGIVE YOU!

Most two-year-olds are beginning to understand that other people have feelings too—and that they can make someone else feel scared or mad or sad. They are also beginning to be able to feel "sorry" for others—and may even give a person a smile or hug to make them feel better.

TRIP

A couple of months later, when Jasmine and Mommy were at the doctor's office, Jasmine laughed, clapped her hands—and smiled at a baby! And the baby smiled back. Then Jasmine sang, "Hi dere lit-tle baby! Lit-tle ba-beeeeeeeeeeeeeeeeeee!" And the baby started to cry.

"Oh! Oh-no! Baby crying! Baby sad!" whispered Jasmine. Then she looked at the baby, smiled, puckered up her lips, and made sweet kissing sounds. And the baby stopped crying, puckered up his lips, and made the same sweet kissing sounds. And that made Jasmine laugh.

Jasmine and Jackson's most favorite baby-sitter was Grandpa. One night, he brought the twins a treat—mini-marshmallows to put in their hot chocolate. Jackson put all his marshmallows in his hot chocolate and watched them melt. Jasmine put all her marshmallows in her mouth and chewed them—a little.

Then she stuck them in Jackson's hair and giggled. Jackson giggled too and sputtered, "Jackie like it!" But when Grandpa cut the icky, sticky marshmallows out of Jackson's hair, Jackson hollered, "Gramp cutted Jackie hair! Jackie mad Gramp!" He hollered until Grandpa gave him a kiss. Then Grandpa said, "Don't put sticky stuff in your hair ever again! Okay?" And the twins said, "Okay, Gramp!" and gave him a big hug.

Twins are not only twins. They are also each other's brother or sister. Like other brothers and sisters, two-year-old twins get mad at each other—and may yell at, hit, or sometimes even bite each other. But most of the time, twins feel very loving and often give each other hugs and kisses.

Two-year-olds are still learning to talk. But now they can say sentences like "She hitted me!" or "When Mommy comed home?" or "Me puts socksies on my footsies." Later on, two-year-olds say words like "hit," "coming," "socks," or "feet" instead of saying words like "hitted," "comed," "socksies," or "footsies."

IT'S NOT FOOTSIES! IT'S TOOTSIES!

ME PUT SOCKSIES ON MY FOOTSIES!

At the playground, Jackson, Hannah, and Zweli liked to watch bugs. One day, Zweli asked, "Where the ants?" Soon, Jackson said, "I seeed ants! I seeed mommy ants, daddy ants, baby ants!" And they all sat still for a very long time—watching the parade of ants crawl across the sidewalk.

Jasmine, Dylan, and Alyssa liked to slide down the slide fast. One day, when Jasmine slid down, Dylan slid down after her and bumped into her.

"Dylan stupid!" Jasmine yelled. "He hitted me!"

"Jassie hurt?" asked Dylan. "Got boo-boo, Jassie?"

"No boo-boo. Okay. Jassie okay," said Jasmine. And they climbed up the slide and slid down fast—again.

Twins—even those who look almost exactly like each other—are never exactly like each other. They may have different friends or like different foods. One might like to scribble with crayons. The other might like to finger-paint. One might be noisy. The other might be quiet.

When two-year-olds call someone "stupid," they don't really know what that word means. But many might know that it's not a nice word. Later on, they do learn that using words like "stupid" or "doo-doo" can make a person—a sister or brother or friend—feel bad or mad. And that helps them try to stop using those kinds of words.

A few weeks later, the twins and Daddy walked all the way to the shoe store. When they finally got there, Jasmine flopped down on the floor and cried, "Jassie no want sneakers!" When Daddy asked her to try on some sneakers, Jasmine kicked her feet, rolled over, pounded her fists, and screamed, "JAS-SIE want goed home—NOW-OOOOOOOOOOOOW!"

She screamed even louder when Daddy said, "Ohhhh, my sweet Jasmine."

But when Jackson said, "Hi sweet Jasmine," and kissed the top of his sister's head, she stopped screaming and whispered, "Nice Jackson." Soon, Jackson had on new sneakers with red racing stripes. Jasmine had on new pink sneakers. After that, they all walked home.

SPINACH IS DELISH!

NO WANT IT! NO WANT IT! NEED COOKIE NOW! NOW!

A tantrum happens when angry feelings "pop out" all at once. When two-year-olds have a tantrum, they are not being bad. Often they don't even know why they feel bad. Or they just don't have the words to say what they want or if they are feeling bad or unhappy or very tired. Once a tantrum is over, everyone usually feels better.

BETTER?

YUP.

When a two-year-old has a tantrum, sometimes brothers or sisters can help. If a sister or brother asks, "Wanna toy?" or says "Hi!" or says the two-year-old's name, or gently pats the two-year-old's head, often, but not always, the two-year-old will stop screaming and kicking and will quiet down—and feel better.

WANNA DUCKIE?

HI!

One winter day, Mommy said, "It's time to go to Hannah's!"

"Why?" asked Jasmine.

"It's her birthday party," said Mommy.

"Why?" asked Jasmine.

"Today's Hannah's special day!" said Mommy.

"Why?" asked Jasmine.

"It's the day she was born," said Mommy.

"Let's go Hannah party!" shouted Jasmine. So they put on their snow boots—and went to the party.

That night, when Jasmine picked up the telephone, she asked, "Who's zat?" "What's that?" she asked when she pointed to a box of spaghetti. "Where kitty go?" she asked when the cat scurried under the couch. "Why you cry?" she asked when Jackson scraped his knee. Jasmine could not stop asking questions.

When two-year-olds ask "why?" often it's because they don't understand why something is happening or why someone is asking them to do something. It's also possible that many two-year-olds ask "why?" over and over again because they want to make sure the person they ask will keep on talking with them.

When two-year-olds ask questions like "what's that?" sometimes they want to know the answer. Other times they're not interested in hearing the answer. Sometimes they don't even wait to listen to the answer. But it's fun for them to ask questions because when they do, people talk to them—and they love talking with other people.

One Sunday when Grandpa was baby-sitting, Jackson ran and told Grandpa, "Gramp! Gramp! She painted!"

"What?" asked Grandpa.

"Jassie! Yellow and red!" said Jackson. "She painted! Up and down! It's pret-ty!"

Grandpa and Jackson ran to the twin's room. Jasmine was still painting red stripes on the wall! There were yellow fingerprints on the wall too.

"Pret-ty, Gramp?" asked Jasmine.

"Jasmine, we don't paint on walls!" said Grandpa.

"I do, Gramp!" said Jasmine.

"Jassie bad!" said Jackson.

"Jasmine's not bad. She's good. She just made a mistake," said Grandpa, "so let's clean it up." And Jasmine, Jackson, and Grandpa washed all of the paint off the wall.

HEY! A BIG RED FIRE TRUCK! I DRAWED A BIG RED FIRE TRUCK! SEE IT? I DID IT!

Many older two-year-olds can say the names of some colors—"red," "yellow," "blue," "green," "purple," or "black." They can say "truck red" when they see a fire truck—or "fire truck red," "big truck," "your truck," "my truck," or "dump truck"—because now they understand that the same thing—a truck, a hat, a dog, or a cat—can come in different colors, sizes, and shapes.

Two-year-old twins—like other two-year-olds—copy the words and sounds all the people around them make, not just the words and sounds their twin makes. Sometimes twins, or any two young children who are with each other a lot, use a few of their own special words to talk to each other—words they have heard each other say a lot. At times, these are words no one else can understand.

TOOPLE BOOP!

GOPPLE BOP?

One morning, Jasmine threw her bear, quilt, chickie, and fire truck out of her crib. Jackson watched and laughed. Then Jasmine put one leg over the side of her crib and began to climb out.

"Oh, no! Oh, my!" said Mommy as she ran in and lifted Jasmine out of her crib. "It's time for a big bed."

Two-year-olds can climb. And many try to climb—and do climb—out of their cribs. When they can do that, it's time for them to sleep in a bed. Some sleep in a bed right away. Others wait for a while and may put a stuffed animal or toy on their bed first—until they feel ready to sleep in a "big bed."

Daddy and Mommy moved two beds into the twins' room. Jackson sat next to his new bed with his doggie, looking at *The Big Dog Book* and singing, "Big boy! Big doggie! Doggie NOT like big-boy bed! NOT!" Jasmine stood up on her new bed, holding her bear and singing, "Big girl! Big bear! Yippy, YIPPY! Bear love big-girl bed!" That night, Jackson slept in his crib. Jasmine slept in her new bed.

THE PIG, THE HORSE, THE COW ALL SAY "OINK."

OINK?

Two-year-olds can't really read words, but they love to be read to and love to pretend to "read" the words. Often they pretend to "read" to their dolls or stuffed animals, or to a brother or sister or friend by making up a story. That's one way they learn to talk in sentences and tell stories.

The next night, when Daddy turned on the vacuum cleaner, Jackson yelled, "Turn OFF—PLEEZE! Gonna eat me ALL up!" And he hid behind Mommy until Daddy turned it off. That night, when Jasmine watched the tub water go down the drain, she yelled, "DON'T wanna goes down dere! Get me OUT—PLEEZE!"

When Daddy told the twins they were way too big to go down the drain or into a vacuum cleaner, they both felt a tiny bit better. A few weeks later, when Daddy vacuumed, Jackson sang, "Jackie go vac! I do it! I vac!" and helped Daddy vacuum. When Jasmine took her bath, she sang, "Bye-bye water! Jassie too big!" and watched the water go down the drain.

Many two-year-olds can't quite understand that they are too big to go down a drain or into a vacuum cleaner or garbage truck or that loud noises—like a siren or a toilet being flushed—can't hurt them. That's why, for a while, many are afraid of loud noises or afraid they can get sucked down a drain or into a machine.

Some older two-year-olds can say as many as six or more words in a row. Now that they can finally say so many words, they say longer sentences like "Go to bakey store! Get a cookie, okay?" or "I want to go with you, okay?" or "I get book daddy me read book, okay?"—sentences that almost everyone can understand.

I GET BOOK.
ME READ BOOK.
ME READ SPIDER BOOK.
I LOVE MY BOOK.
I LOVE MY MOON BOOK TOO.

JACKIE GO VAC-VAC!

WHOOOOOoooooooooooooo

One afternoon, Zweli put on a pirate hat, Hannah put on a hard hat, and Jasmine put on a firefighter's hat. Dylan put on a top hat, Alyssa put on a gold crown, and Jackson put on a clown hat. And Alyssa and Jackson climbed into a big box.

Zweli sang, "Wheels on da bus go round and round!"

Alyssa yelled, "My yellow bus big! I driving it!"

Jasmine drew big blue dots all over the box. "Look! Big wheels!" she shouted.

"Lots of wheels!" hollered Hannah. "One, two, three, and more wheels!"

Jackson sang, "Bye-bye-toot-toot!"—and waved good-bye.

> I'M GRANNY! I LOVE GRANNY'S SLIPPERS ON ME!

Two-year-olds love to play. When older two-year-olds "dress up" and put on Grandma's slippers and pretend to be a grandma, they are trying to find out what it's like to be a grandma. When they climb into a box and pretend it's a castle, they are trying to find out what it's like to be in a castle.

> I WANT A CHEESE PIZZA! SEND A BIG BAG CHIPS!

Two-year-olds love to talk when they are playing—even when they are alone or on the phone, even when no one is talking to them. "I want a cheese pizza! Send a big bag chips!" they might say. They often sound very bossy because knowing and saying so many new words is very exciting—and that makes them blurt out the words as loud and as fast as they can.

One day, Jackson poured water in his new potty and put a flower in it. That same day, Jasmine sat on her new potty and looked at a book. For a while, neither Jackson nor Jasmine used their potty to pee or poop. Then one day, Jasmine yelled, "Go potty!," grabbed *The Bear Book,* pulled down her diaper, sat down—and peed in her potty.

"I a big girl!" said Jasmine. Her mommy gave Jasmine a hug and underpants with purple dinosaurs on them—and Jasmine smiled a big smile.

When girls use a potty to pee, they sit down. When boys use a potty to pee, at first, most sit down. After a while, boys stand up to pee. When boys and girls use a potty to poop, they both sit down. When they can finally use a potty, they feel proud because they can now do what older kids and grown-ups do. Some learn to use a potty before their third birthdays. Some learn after their third birthdays.

Many, but not all, two-year-olds know the difference between boys' and girls' bodies. What some may know is that having a vagina is what makes a child a girl—and having a penis is what makes a child a boy.

Weeks later, Jackson pulled down his diaper, sat down on his potty—and peed in his potty. Jasmine clapped.

"Pee-pee in potty! I a big boy!" shouted Jackson. His mommy gave him a hug and underpants with lions and tigers on them— and Jackson smiled a big smile.

The morning of their third birthday, the twins and Mommy baked two cakes. Jasmine put purple jelly beans on her cake. Jackson put red, white, and blue sprinkles on his cake. They both stuck three big candles in their cakes.

At their party, Jackson said, "YES!" when Grandpa said it was time to blow out the candles. But when Jasmine blew them out before Jackson could, he cried, "NO Jassie!"

Grandpa lit the candles again. This time, Jackson and Jasmine both blew out the candles and shouted, "Happy birthday!" Then they hugged each other, fell in a heap—and hugged again! On their third birthday, Jackson and Jasmine were **3**. Jackson and Jasmine were GROWING UP!

WATCH ME! I'M A DANCER! I CAN TIPTOE!

CAN I HAVE THE BALL, PLEASE?

OKAY.

By age three, many young children no longer say "No!" as much and say "Yes!" a lot. And sometimes they even use words like "Stop!" or "That hurt me!" to say they are angry, instead of hitting back. Many have also learned to say "Please," "Thank you!" and "Okay." And by age three, they can say about 1,000 words, even though they don't know what all of them mean—yet.

By age three, many young children can do all kinds of new things. Many can walk backwards and on tiptoe, kick a ball, build a small tower, climb up a slide, eat with a spoon, draw a circle, take off their pants, use a potty, wash their hands, ride a tricycle, play with and be a friend, have 20 teeth, count "1, 2, 3!"—and sing almost all the words to "Happy Birthday!"

I HAVE 1, 2, 3, 20 TEETH!

YOU ARE GROWING UP! THAT IS WAY COOL, MAN!

THANK YOU

FOR SHARING YOUR EXPERTISE AND AFFECTION FOR 2-YEAR-OLDS WITH US!

Rosa Aguirre, consultant, Somerville, MA

Naomi S. Baron, Ph.D., professor of linguistics, American University, Washington, D.C.

Marjorie Beegley, Ph.D., senior research associate, Child Development Unit, Children's Hospital, Boston, MA; assistant professor of pediatrics, Harvard Medical School, Boston, MA

Sarah Birss, M.D., child analyst and pediatrician, Cambridge, MA

Kate Buttenwieser, M.S.W., social worker, Children's Hospital, Boston, MA

Deborah Chamberlain, M.S., research associate, Norwood, MA

Kathy Shelton Clem, Ed.D., literacy specialist, Hanover, NH

Sally Crissman, science educator, Shady Hill School, Cambridge, MA

Jennifer Ganger, Ph.D., visiting professor of psychology, University of Pittsburgh, Pittsburgh, PA; supervisor, MIT Twins Study, Massachusetts Institute of Technology, Cambridge, MA

Bill Harris, grandparent, Cambridge, MA

Emily Berkman Harris, M.D., pediatrician, New York, NY

Hilary Grand Harris, parent, New York, NY

Margot Kaplan-Sanoff, Ed.D., assistant clinical professor of pediatrics; codirector, Healthy Steps, Boston University Medical Center, Boston, MA

Ellen Kelley, director, The Cambridge-Ellis School, Cambridge, MA

Elizabeth A. Levy, children's book author, New York, NY

Alicia Lieberman, Ph.D., professor of medical psychology, University of California at San Francisco, San Francisco, CA

Linda C. Mayes, M.D., Arnold Gesell professor of psychiatry/pediatrics and psychology, Yale University Child Study Center, New Haven, CT

Armanda Mela, grandparent, Brighton, MA

Audrey Heffernan Meyer, parent, New York, NY

Janet Patterson, kindergarten teacher, Shady Hill School, Cambridge, MA

Jeree Pawl, Ph.D., director, Infant Parent Program, University of California at San Francisco, San Francisco, CA

Laura Riley, M.D., obstetrician/gynecologist, director, OB/GYN Infectious Diseases, Massachusetts General Hospital, Boston, MA

Carol Sepkoski, Ph.D., developmental psychologist, Cambridge, MA

Karen Shorr, M.A.T., prekindergarten teacher, The Brookwood School, Manchester, MA

Lauren A. Smith, M.D., M.P.H., Department of Pediatrics, Boston Medical Center, Boston University School of Medicine, Boston, MA

Beatrice Stratter, parent, Brighton, MA

Edward Z. Tronick, Ph.D., chief, Child Development Unit, Children's Hospital, Boston, MA; associate professor of pediatrics, Harvard Medical School, Boston, MA

Pamela Meyer Zuckerman, M.D., pediatrician, Brookline, MA